Enid

The Beautiful Pattern

Illustrated by Pam Storey

This edition printed in 2000

Published by
Grandreams Limited
435-437 Edgware Road
Little Venice
London W2 1TH

Printed in Indonesia

Once upon a time there was a little boy called Morris. He went to school, and he was very good at all his lessons - except drawing. You should have seen the pictures he drew!

"Well, really, Morris, I don't know if this drawing is meant to be a dustbin, a house, an elephant, or a banana!" his teacher said one day. "And is this the best pattern you can make for me? Well, I really do think you might have done better than this!"

The children often drew patterns in the drawing-lesson, and coloured the patterns they made. Sometimes they were quite simple ones, like this:

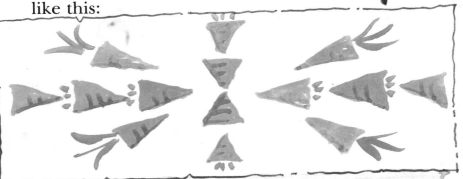

or prettier ones like this:

They could draw what patterns they liked, and they could use the letters of the alphabet or figures or anything they pleased, so long as they made a really pretty pattern. It was fun to chalk the patterns.

Poor Morris could never think of a good pattern at all. Once he thought it would be a good thing to do a pattern of aeroplanes, but when he drew them they looked rather like birds with no head and two tails - so it wasn't such a good pattern after all!

One day the teacher gave her children some homework to do over the weekend.

"I want you to think of a really lovely pattern," she said - "the sort of pattern that would look nice on our wallpaper. Now do think of an unusual and beautiful one, draw it out on a sheet of paper and then colour it."

Poor Morris! When he got home and sat down with his sheet of paper and a pencil, do you suppose he could think of any pattern at all? Not one!

I expect you could think of plenty, and draw them beautifully - but you are cleverer than Morris.

"It's a shame!" thought Morris, leaning his head on his hand. "I can do sums well - and I'm always top in history - but I just CAN'T draw!"

"Morris! Whatever are you looking so worried about?" called his mother. "Don't sit and look so gloomy. Put on your hat and coat and go out into the snow. The sun is shining, and it will do you good to go and play."

So Morris put on his hat and coat and out he went into the snow. He thought he would go to the little wood nearby. It was a lovely place, because the trees grew very close together and made it rather exciting and mysterious.

Off he went, and into the little wood. And there he saw something he had never seen before. It was a little house made of snow! It had snow walls, a snow chimney, windows made of little sheets of ice, and no door at all - just an opening.

"What a dear little house!" thought Morris. "I wonder who made it? Surely no one can live there?"

He went to the house. He peeped in at the window, but he could see nothing through the ice-panes. He went to the doorway and peeped through the opening.

And inside he saw a long-bearded brownie, very busy papering the snow walls of his house!

"Good gracious!" said Morris. "Are you really a brownie? I didn't think you lived anywhere except in books. Are you real?"

"Well, what a question to ask anyone!" said the brownie crossly. "What a funny boy you are! Do you think I'm a dream, or something?"

"Well, you might be," said Morris. "I say - what a lovely wallpaper! Where did you get it from?"

"I made it myself," said the brownie. "I did the pattern myself too. Do you like it?"

"It's a marvellous pattern," said Morris, looking at it. "How did you think of it? I can never think of patterns like this."

"Oh, I don't think of them," said the brownie, his green eyes shining as he looked at Morris. "I just go out and look for them!"

"Look for patterns!" cried Morris. "Well, I wish I could do that! I'm always getting into trouble at school because I can't do patterns. Where do you see your patterns when you go to look for them?"

"Well, last summer I made a beautiful pattern of daisy-heads," said the brownie. "Quite easy too, it was - just a little round middle with petals all round it. I made a most beautiful wallpaper of that. And another time I went out into the woods and found some green bracken just beginning to grow, and to uncurl its green fingers - and I made a pattern of that too."

"What lovely things to make patterns from!" said Morris. "But this wallpaper of yours hasn't daisies or bracken on. It's not a flower-pattern at all. What is it? I'm sure you've made it up."

"No, I haven't," said the brownie. "I got this pattern from the snow."

Morris stared at him in surprise. "But I've never seen the snow in patterns like that!" he said.

"Ah, that's because you haven't looked carefully enough at the snow-crystals," said the brownie. "Each snow-crystal is a little pattern in itself - didn't you know that?"

"No, I didn't," said Morris. "I don't even know what you mean."

"Whatever do they teach you at school?" said the brownie, in astonishment. "Why, at the brownie school I went to we all learnt about the beauty of snow-crystals. Well, I'll tell you. You've seen snowflakes falling, haven't you?"

"Of course," said Morris. "They are falling again now."

"Well, each snowflake is made up of snow-crystals," said the brownie. "And now, here is a funny thing - every snow-crystal is different, and yet it is the same in one thing - it is six-sided! Shall we go and catch some snowflakes and look at them through my magic glass? Then you will see what I mean."

So out they went into the wood, where the
snow was beginning to fall quite thickly. The
little brownie took with him a piece of black
velvet, and he caught a snowflake on this. Then
he took out a round glass in a frame and made
Morris look at the snowflake through the glass -
and to the boy's great surprise he saw that the
flake was made up of snow-crystals lightly
joined together, and every single crystal had six
sides to it! Not one of them had four sides or
five sides or seven sides - each had six. They
were all quite different, but they were very
beautiful!

"How perfectly lovely!" said Morris, astonished. "Oh, I do like them! Look - here is one rather like the pattern on your wallpaper! No wonder you managed to get such a pretty pattern, brownie - why, there are dozens of different patterns for you to use in one snowflake!"

"Yes," said the brownie. "I chose one the other day, and drew it out on my paper, then coloured it. Don't you think it will look sweet on the walls of my new snow-house?"

"I do," said Morris. "You've given me such a good idea, brownie! I'm going straight home now to make a snow-crystal pattern. That's my homework this weekend. I ought to get top marks, for I am sure no one else will have such a lovely pattern as mine!"

"Well, good-bye," said the brownie, going back into his house. "I must go on with my papering. Come back on Monday afternoon and tell me if you got top marks."

Morris ran home. He burst into the sitting-room and told his mother all about the brownie and his magic glass.

"I wish I had asked him to lend it to me," he said. "Then I could have chosen the prettiest snow-crystal to do - I'm afraid I shan't remember one very well."

"I have a kind of magic glass you can see through," said his mother. "It's Daddy's magnifying glass! It makes things look much bigger when you look through it. I'll get it."

She fetched it, and Morris went outside to catch a snowflake on his coat-sleeve and looked at it through the magnifying glass. Goodness, how lovely the six-sided crystals were! Like stars or flowers, very small and perfect.

"I'll make a pattern just like that one there," said Morris to himself, and he looked at the crystal very carefully indeed to get it into his memory. Then he went indoors and got his sheet of paper. He drew a row of six-sided crystals, then another and another and another, till he had a whole page of them. Then he coloured them beautifully and took his pattern to his mother.

"How marvellous!" she cried. "This is the loveliest pattern you have ever done! How I would like to have it for my wallpaper!"

Well, as you can guess, Morris got top marks for it, and the teacher pinned the pattern up on the wall for everyone to see. Morris could hardly wait for the afternoon to come, because he so badly wanted to tell the brownie that he had done a beautiful snow-crystal and got top marks! He looked out of the window. The sun was shining brightly and felt quite hot on his hand.

Morris rushed off to the wood as soon as he could - but oh, what a disappointment! The sun had melted the snow, and there was no little snow-house to be seen! There was only a wet pile of paper on which Morris could just see the pattern the brownie had made.